Over Land Or Sea…
A Poetry Yearbook

Suzanne McDonough

Published in 2009 by New Generation Publishing

Dedication

To Joesam - a sturdy Plymouth Pilot used for
fishing locally, a well- respected boat crewed
by Geoff and Andy-
All your hard work inspired me!
Thanks!

Acknowledgements

To the editors of the following publications in which some of these poems first appeared: Reach Poetry – A Poetry Society Landmark magazine Indigo Dreams Press, All Our Days Anthology, Special Places Anthology

Thanks to Peter Mortimer Author, Poet, Playwright, and Editor, whose works have encouraged me including
Last Of The Hunters, Broke Through Britain and 100 Days On Holy Island.

Contents

My Soul Mate

I close my eyes
And think of you
And all our time together
I know I have found my soul mate
A best friend to love forever.

No matter where we go
We are together as one
Over land or sea…
Miles apart
We were always meant to be,
My love
My chosen one!

A Coastal Retreat

The day was dark and uneventful.
The weather had deteriorated,
And torrential rain fell from heavy black clouds.
Sleet tapped on the window
And swirled around the garden
A thin white blanket covered the ground
Crocuses were lost in the gentle snow
As daffodils greeted the land graciously
In the roaring noise of the wind.

The outlook changed day by day
But the lighthouse remained the same.
The sky was reflected in the sea
A gloomy grey and a brilliant blue,
And, this was the view
From a small wooden window overlooking the sea.

JANUARY – The perfect sunrise appears over the headland. The breaking dawn gives way to a new day.

Lead Me To The Shore

Gazing over the fields and fences
Heading for the trees,
Looking straight ahead
Hair blowing in the breeze,
Winding tracks,
Sloping tracks,
Many treasures to adore
Violets and seaside pansies
Lead me to the shore.

Footprints left along the way
Only a few people pass,
Could there be wild rabbits hiding in the grass?
The smell of the sea guides me
Just a few paces more,
Violets and seaside pansies
Lead me to the shore.

FEBRUARY...

Sea

I can see you
I can hear you
I can smell you
And when the tide is in I can touch you
You are the sea.
The great mass of salt water
Smaller than the ocean
But larger than a lake.

Ridges move across you
Arching and breaking on the shore
The pull of the sun and moon change you
From high to low you rise and fall,
Showing the sea bed
The seaweed
The seashells
I feel the sea breeze
And see change.

MARCH…

St-Mary's Lighthouse

Tall and white
Shining bright through the night
Keeping boats off jagged rocks
Watching over wayward flocks.
Covered in mist, sea fret, and fog
Watching over wayward seadogs
Standing proud for all to see
Watching over you and me.
Keeping guard while the village sleeps
Watching over those who weep
Disaster strikes lives may be lost
But the lighthouse guides at any cost
Watching over the coast and shoreline
Protecting the region and the Tyne.

St-Mary's Lighthouse is situated on the north east coast at Whitley Bay.
There has been a lighthouse on St-Mary's Island since mediaeval times,
and the present lighthouse was opened in 1898.
It marks the half-distance between Blyth and the Tyne.

APRIL…

Storm Clouds

Silver grey mist hovers
Across the open land,
Pearls of rain dance in the wind
As if hand in hand.

The foghorn sounds
Keeping watch over the open bay,
Many boats will pass the coast
Today on their merry way.

As the sky darkens shadows form
A rumble comes from the sea,
Thunder way in the distance
Lightning flashes in the trees.

The foghorn gets louder and louder
And the thunder roars
Waves crash on the jagged rocks
The rain just pours, and pours.

MAY...

What A Special Place To Be

The deepest darkest midnight sky
Engulfs the world as time goes by,
The beach is so peaceful
The sea is so still,
The stars shine brightly
In the air there's a chill.

The waves lap gently around our feet
Here together,
Not another soul shall we meet.

Shells glitter in the soft sand
At this moment you take my hand,
Standing close we look out to sea
What a special place to be!

It all looks so different in daylight hours
But nothing can compare
With this secret of ours,
We will look back one day and remember
All the good times we had here
From March to November!

JUNE – A vibrant orange sunset unfolds against a cloudless summer sky.

Reunited

Umbrellas line the beach across the bay
A sea of white domes
Cascade down to the waters edge
People are scattered innocently here and there
Boats sway gently along the waterline
Cool clear turquoise water beacons
Softly rippled by a slight breeze
Another, relaxing day in a place of utter bliss.

Pathways made of rounded stone
Twist and turn
And gradually we learn
To find our way around the village.

Friendly and familiar faces appear
And time passes with such ease
The pace is slow and welcoming
And this is all that we need.
As the sun goes down across the bay
We look forward to a brand new day
Reunited.

JULY...

Blue Skies

The sound of Lapwings and the sea
Bring me back to reality
And, I cherish all I have today
A special place come what may
.

I have a love for you to see me through
The darkest ever days.

My heart is yours, and yours alone
And, filled with warmth I head for home
Awaiting, your return.

AUGUST...

Seaton Delaval Hall

Here stands a magnificent structure built of dark grey cold stone.
A weather beaten monument streaked with purple and brown.
Its towers and columns reach up to the never-ending sky.
This wonderful winter palace is encapsulated by a gnarled oak forest.

Empty eyes watch from large windows high in gigantic walls.

And, the wind howls among the balustraded battlements.

As the sun goes down light forms grey shadows which magically
disappear into the dense woodland.
The watery winter sun sets over open fields
While a crisp wind cuts through the hedgerow.

Singing spirits stir as the north-easterly wind blows.
Laughter echoes across the ploughed land
Sweeping the countryside far and wide
Only to be carried out to sea on an invisible wave.

SEPTEMBER...

Harvest-Time

The sea beckoned beyond the hedgerow
Silently accepting the day.
The field was vast and open
And, the cool summer breeze swept across the sweet scented grassland.

The painted wooden 'vardo'stood proudly in the shade
Displaying its ornate carvings and painted designs,
Decorated with gold leaf, and a multiple of finds.

Gypsy stood nearby munching on fresh hay
Gleaming white in the hazy light,
Then I knew it was a magical day
Mirela had returned,
My Romany friend to stay.

OCTOBER...

Not Alone

A private cove
With steep steep steps
Jagged rocks
And a shingle shore
A sandy bay
And, sea washed seams of coal.

Driftwood washes in with the tide
And when the storm does subside
Footsteps appear in the sand
Across a deserted beach.

NOVEMBER...

Contemplation

White foam covers the causeway
Floating in rock pools
And clinging to well washed pebbles
As the tide turns.

Cut off from the mainland
The lighthouse merges into the soft grey evening sky.
A silver reflection cascades forming a shadow on the sea,
As the day closes.

DECEMBER – Heavy storms send wild waves to wash away the winter blues.

Joesam
For Dad Geoff

Leaving the harbour
The blue fishing boats engine chugs in harmony
With the breaking waves.

In deeper water lines are cast
And troubles of the day
Drift away
To long lost distant shores,
Across the open sea.

Over Land Or Sea…